My "t" Sound Box®

WRITTEN BY JANE BELK MONCURE • ILLUSTRATED BY REBECCA THORNBURGH

The Child's World®
childsworld.com

Published by The Child's World®
1980 Lookout Drive • Mankato, MN 56003-1705
800-599-READ • www.childsworld.com

ISBN HARDCOVER: 9781503823235
ISBN PAPERBACK: 9781503831452
LCCN: 2017960385

Printed in the United States of America
PA02430

A NOTE TO PARENTS AND EDUCATORS:

Magic moon machines and five fat frogs are just a few of
the fun things you can share with children by reading books
with them. Reading aloud helps children in so many ways!
It introduces them to new words, motivates them to develop
their own reading skills, and expands their attention span
and listening abilities. So it's important to find time each day
to share a book or two . . . or three!

As you read with young children, you can help develop
their understanding of how print works by talking about the
parts of the book—the cover, the title, the illustrations, and the
words that tell the story. As you read, use your finger to point
to each word, modeling a gentle sweep from left to right.

Simple word games help develop important prereading
skills, including an understanding of rhyme and alliteration
(when words share the same beginning sound, such as "six"
and "sand"). Try playing with words from a book you've
just shared: "What other words start with the same sound
as moon?" "Cat and hat, do those words rhyme?" The
possibilities are endless—and so are the rewards!

My "t" Sound Box®

Little 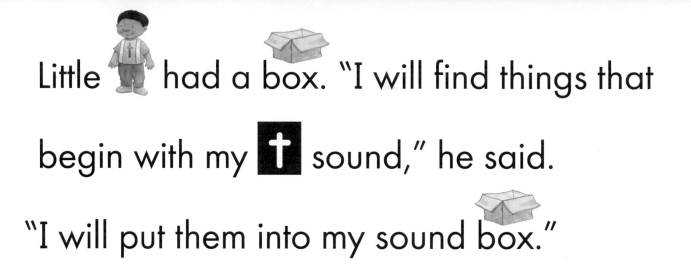 had a box. "I will find things that begin with my **t** sound," he said.

"I will put them into my sound box."

"I like toys. I will look for toys."

Little  found a toy train on a train track. Did he put the toy train and the track into his box? He did.

Little  found a toy tractor. Did he put the tractor into the box with the toy train and the track? He did.

Then Little  found a truck. He drove

the truck up, up, up a tall mountain.

He drove to the top, the very tip-top!

At the top of the tall mountain, he found two turtles. Did he put the two turtles into his box? He did.

Then he found a toad. Did he put

the toad into the box? He did.

Now the box was so full that he could

not see over the top. He tripped!

He tumbled down, down, down the mountain.

He tumbled into a turkey. Turkey feathers flew!

So Little  made a

turkey-feather hat.

He and the turkey tap-danced together.

Little  found a tambourine. He tapped the tambourine. Tap, tap, tap. Tap, tap, tap.

Little  , the turkey, and the
 toad tap-danced some more.

Then Little  put all of his things into the box.

Suddenly, Little heard a terrific

noise! He ran into a tent.

When he looked out, he saw a tiger!

The tiger opened its mouth. The tiger's mouth had many teeth.

"I have a loose tooth," said the tiger. "Please pull out my tooth."

So Little  pulled out the tooth.

"Thank you," said the tiger.

Then Little  and the tiger went inside the tent. They played with all the toys in the box.

They had a terrific time!

Little 's Word List

tambourine

toad

train

teeth

toy

truck

tent

track

turkey

tiger

tractor

turtle

Other Words with Little

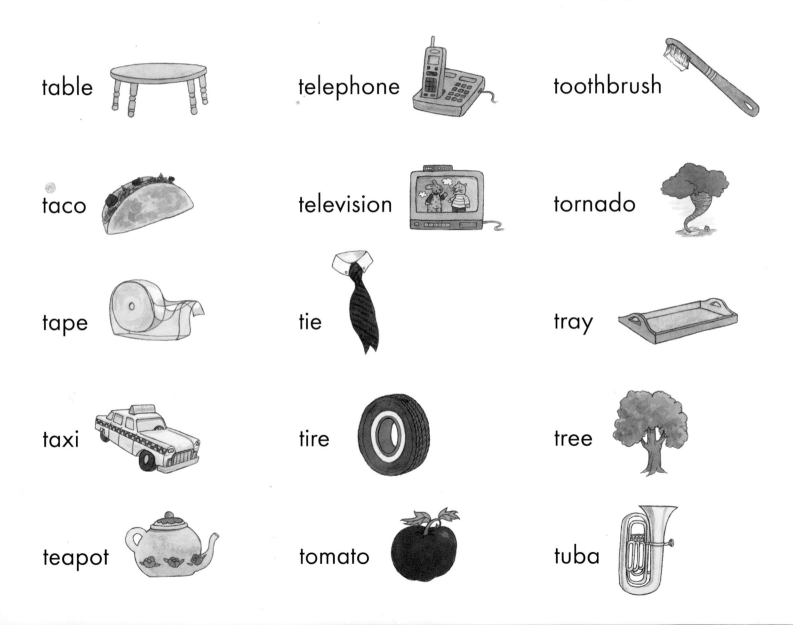

table

telephone

toothbrush

taco

television

tornado

tape

tie

tray

taxi

tire

tree

teapot

tomato

tuba

More to Do!

You can trace your hands and feet to make silly turkeys! Ask a friend to help with the tracing.

What you need:

- brown construction paper
- red, yellow, and orange construction paper
- markers

Directions:

1. First, take off your shoes and have your helper trace your feet on the brown paper. Then cut out your foot shapes.

2. Glue the two shapes together at the heels as they are shown in the picture. Be sure not to glue the toes together! These brown shapes will be the turkey's body.

3. Place your hands on the piece of yellow paper. Be sure to spread your fingers out! Ask your helper to trace all around your hands and fingers. Do the same thing on the red and orange pieces of paper. Now cut out your hand shapes.

4. Glue the hands to the back of the brown foot shapes. The hand shapes make the feathers!

5. Draw two eyes and a beak on the brown paper. Now your turkey is finished!

About the Author

Best-selling author Jane Belk Moncure (1926–2013) wrote more than 300 books throughout her teaching and writing career. After earning a master's degree in early childhood education from Columbia University, she became one of the pioneers in that field. In 1956, she helped form the Virginia Association for Early Childhood Education, which established the first statewide standards for teachers of young children.

Inspired by her work in the classroom, Mrs. Moncure's books became standards in primary education, and her name was recognized across the country. Her success was reflected not only in her books' popularity with parents, children, and educators, but also by numerous awards, including the 1984 C. S. Lewis Gold Medal Award.

About the Illustrator

Rebecca Thornburgh lives in a pleasantly spooky old house in Philadelphia. If she's not at her drawing table, she's reading—or singing with her band, called Reckless Amateurs. Rebecca has one husband, two daughters, and two silly dogs.